Colette & the Princess

COLETTE AND

THE PRINCESS

LOUIS SLOBODKIN

E. P. DUTTON & CO., INC.

NEW YORK

j S6343co

For *Naomi*
with love

When the fretful Princess Pauline chose the little mountain town of Grasse as the place for a good, quiet rest, she demanded Absolute Silence throughout the village.

The good Mayor saw to it that bundles of hay were tied around the iron shoes of horses and donkeys, that all the window and door hinges were oiled, that cowbells were removed from cows, and that everything else he could think of was silenced.

His little daughter Colette made woolen slippers to wear over her wooden shoes, and knitted a tiny woolen muzzle of pink wool for her kitten Chou Chou.

And all the people tried to maintain Absolute Silence too. They either said nothing at all, or spoke in whispers.

Well, as you can imagine, this ridiculous situation just couldn't go on very long. You will of course want to find out for yourself what happens to rescue the good-mannered people of Grasse from Princess Pauline's silly demands, but if you have already suspected that Colette and her little kitten Chou Chou have something to do with it — you're right.

Princesses are not always beautiful, delicate little girls with dainty little noses, long golden tresses, and soft, sweet voices.

Sometimes they are grown-up ladies who eat too many creamed tarts and have large red noses, graying hair, and loud, harsh voices.

Princess Pauline was that kind of princess.

She was middle-aged, rather stout, and her stringy hair was gray under the golden wig she always wore. No one . . . no matter how polite . . . could say she was beautiful or that she spoke softly.

The Princess Pauline was downcast. She had the vapours (whatever that may be) and a sore throat. She had had unpleasant arguments with everyone.

So her doctor advised her . . . after feeling her pulse

7

. . . and looking at her outstretched tongue, to go down to the south of France to the little mountain town of Grasse for a good, quiet rest.

"It is very important that you rest, that there be absolute silence . . . and that you take one of these pink sugar pills every four hours," said the doctor.

Then he snapped his medicine bag shut and went off to see the old Duchess of Arno, who had bitten the smallest finger of her right hand (by mistake) as she ate a very large peach that morning.

The whole town of Grasse made preparations for the coming of Princess Pauline. A message had come that the Princess must have absolute quiet.

The Mayor of Grasse read the message to the people of the town, and then told them that during the visit of the Royal Princess a new set of laws dealing with silence would be posted in the town square.

He asked the people of Grasse to please obey these laws, and the people of Grasse did obey. They made soft, felt slippers to wear over their hobnailed boots and wooden shoes so that they would not clatter on the pavement.

They tied great bundles of straw around the iron shoes of their horses and donkeys for the same reason.

All cowbells were removed from the necks of cows.

All knockers on doors were either removed from the doors or padded.

8

All windows, door hinges, weathervanes, and cartwheels were very well oiled so they would not squeak.

All milkmaids, fish peddlers, and all other peddlers
stopped shouting their wares in the market place and
along the streets.

The blacksmith stopped pounding his anvil.

The carpenter stopped sawing wood and hammering
nails.

The baker stopped pounding dough.

The shoemaker stopped tapping shoes.

Even the candlemaker stopped dipping candles for
fear the drops of tallow would make a noise.

9

All church bells and school bells were stilled.

All the children stopped bouncing their balls against the walls and on the streets.

Dogs, and even cats, were muzzled so they would not bark or meow. And bags were tied around the mouths of the horses and donkeys so they would not neigh or bray.

At last, on the day before the Princess came, complete silence reigned in the town of Grasse. Yes, all the citizens of Grasse had willingly obeyed the laws of silence, all except one person.

That one person was the wife of the Mayor of Grasse.

"How can I cook in silence?" she protested to the

Mayor at supper that day. "How can I chop the onion for the stew?"

"Crush the onion gently . . . quietly," whispered the Mayor. "And please don't shout. Whisper."

"How can I slice the vegetables for the soup in silence?" asked the Mayor's wife in a hoarse whisper.

"Cook the vegetables whole in the soup," answered the Mayor.

"And the herbs . . . how can I pound and crush the herbs to flavor the food?"

"We will do without herbs to flavor the food during the Princess' visit," answered the Mayor. "And please whisper quietly when you speak."

"Bah!" snorted the Mayor's wife in a whisper. "No herbs? . . . Whole vegetables for the soup? . . . Gently crushed onions? . . . Bah!"

"Yes . . . yes," whispered the Mayor. "That is the law of the land."

Little Colette, the Mayor's only daughter, quietly sipped her soup. She had never seen a real princess before and she looked forward to the royal visit. She had even dreamed about the Princess Pauline.

During the past few days she had knitted a nice, soft pair of woolen slippers to be worn over her little wooden shoes. (Colette had learned to knit when she was very young . . . Now she was seven.) And she had knitted a tiny muzzle of pink wool for her kitten Chou Chou.

Chou Chou did not like to wear the muzzle. She tried

11

to get it off with her forepaws. But Colette had tied it on with a pretty pink ribbon, and it stayed on.

Colette was a quiet little girl, and for her it was easy to obey the laws of silence. But she knew it would be more difficult for her mother.

The Mayor's wife was one of the best cooks in the town of Grasse. She cooked cheerfully and with gusto. She would rattle and slam her pots and pans and knives

about as she prepared the stew for which she was famous. And after noisily chopping up her vegetables and all the secret things she used in the stew, she would wash up the knives, spoons, and bowls she had used . . . and then would burst into song as the delicious smell of her stew filled the kitchen.

Colette knew her mother could not cook in silence.

12

On the following morning, just before the Princess Pauline was due to arrive, all the grownups and all the children of Grasse gathered along the road to the Old Palace, where the Princess would live during her visit. They stood silently, holding huge bouquets of flowers.

With a great cracking of whips, rattle of harness, creaking of wheels, and clatter of hooves, the royal

coach, bearing the Princess, crashed into the town of Grasse!

It was the loudest noise anyone had ever heard in that usually quiet town.

Little Colette, peeking out from behind her bouquet of flowers, could not see the Princess Pauline through the window of the golden coach. She could hardly see the beautiful golden coach at all. The Princess Pauline ordered her coach to stop. She looked at the silent citizens of Grasse.

"What is this?" she shouted. "Is this treason? Is this the way to greet your Royal Princess? . . . Where is the Mayor of this village?"

The Mayor of Grasse, Colette's father, ran forward and bowed deeply to the Princess.

"Your Royal Highness," he whispered, "I am the Mayor of Grasse."

"What then fails your people?" shouted the Princess. "Why do they stand here silent as goons? Are they not happy to see my Royal Presence? Why are there no cheers of greeting? And you, sir Mayor, why do you whisper? . . . Speak up!"

"Your Royal Highness," whispered the Mayor, "the royal message you sent said that absolute silence is needed for your royal health . . . The citizens of Grasse are deeply honored and delighted to greet your Royal Highness. But they greet you in silence . . . They are obeying the new laws that I have passed. All will be silent in Grasse during your visit."

"Oh," said the Princess. "Very good . . . very good . . . Yes, I do need silence . . . absolute silence. But perhaps the citizens of Grasse may be allowed to shout one 'hurrah' to show their great joy at my safe arrival."

"Yes, your Royal Highness," whispered the Mayor. Then he turned to the citizens of Grasse. "One cheer for the Princess Pauline," he said in a loud whisper.

"Hurrah," whispered the people of Grasse as loudly as they dared.

Then Princess Pauline waved her royal hand and the great golden coach rolled on.

The Old Palace, where the Princess would live during her visit, had belonged to her great-grandfather

Prince Gargle the Great. And for these many years no one had lived there. The palace gardens were sadly neglected. They were just a wild mass of vines, weeds, and thistles. So the Princess sent a message to the Mayor of Grasse the next morning. The message said that the Royal Princess Pauline would tour the town and choose some spot under one of the many trees that shaded Grasse for her morning repose.

The spot she chose must be for her private use alone. And she repeated there must be silence . . . Absolute Silence!

That morning, little Colette went out to play (as was her custom) right after breakfast. She carried her kitten Chou Chou and some toys with her to play house under her favorite tree. Little Colette's favorite tree was a big spreading oak that shaded one far corner of the town square. From the place under the tree where Colette always sat and knitted or played, she could look out across the valley to the bright blue sea. And her

17

tree stood far from the road so no one else ever came to disturb Colette at her little game.

This morning she pretended that Chou Chou was a little baby. She had wrapped the kitten up in an old shawl and was just rocking her to sleep when Princess Pauline . . . riding in a great golden sedan chair carried by two huge chairmen . . . came into the square.

The Princess was accompanied by the Mayor of Grasse, her doctor, and her many servants.

The Mayor had already pointed out the many fine shaded spots all over the town which the Princess could use for her morning repose.

He led her to a place where the prettiest flowers grew . . . to another where the sun rose from the east, and to another where it set in the west. He pointed out a place where one could see the distant Alps on a clear morning, and yet another where one could have the best view of the azure sea.

But the Princess Pauline found none of them to her liking. This place was too draughty . . . This one had too much sun, that one too little. . . .

The Mayor had avoided showing the Princess the town square because it was the center of town life.

It was to the square that all the housewives came every morning to do their marketing. And it was here that the old men of the town gathered to discuss the important topics of the day . . . such as the price of hogs and other weighty subjects.

But at last the Mayor led the Princess and her doctor and her servants into the square. There was no other place left in Grasse to show the Princess.

Many housewives of Grasse were doing their marketing in the square that day. They were not very happy marketing in whispers.

If one whispered, "How much is that not-very-good-looking goat cheese today?" . . . and the cheese merchant whispered back, "Two francs a kilo" . . . one could not very well cry out in a loud horrified voice, "Two francs! . . . it's not worth more than one."

Whispering a reply like that did not sound very convincing.

So most of the time, the housewives would just nod at something marked three francs and hold up two fingers to show they would pay only two francs.

And all through the market, housewives and merchants just glared at each other, shaking their heads as they waved their fingers in the air.

And the old men who sat on the low stone wall that surrounded the square just whispered about the important topics of the day. One would whisper, "Hogs." Another would sadly shrug his shoulders and thrust out his hand, palm down, just a few inches above the ground.

That meant the price of hogs was too low.

That, too, was not a very happy way to carry on an important discussion.

19

Therefore, none of the citizens of Grasse were any happier than the Princess when the Mayor led her into the square. As she sulked behind the curtains of her sedan chair, the Mayor whispered through her curtains about the history of the town square of Grasse.

Suddenly the big chairman who was carrying the front end of the sedan chair stumbled over an old stone that stuck up from the pavement.

"What is it? . . . What has happened? . . . What is it?" cried the Princess as she angrily poked her head out from behind her curtains.

"That stone," whispered the Mayor, "is said to have been placed here in our square by the Romans almost two thousand years ago . . . It marks the spot where the Battle of the Cabbages was fought . . ."

"That's it," shouted the Princess, interrupting him.

"That's what, your Royal Highness?" whispered the Mayor.

"That's the spot . . . that is the very spot I shall use for my morning repose," shouted the Princess Pauline.

She was pointing her royal finger at the far corner of the square to little Colette's favorite oak tree.

"Yes, your Royal Highness," whispered the Mayor sadly. He knew how dearly Colette loved that tree.

"Hurry, carry me there," shouted the Princess to her chairmen.

The Princess' chairmen ran across the square with the curtains of the sedan chair flapping wildly in the breeze. Their great boots clattered on the pavement. The Mayor, the Princess' personal doctor, and her servants raced after them.

When they reached Colette's favorite tree in the far corner of the square, the chairmen set the sedan chair down with a slight bump.

Little Colette jumped to her feet, still cradling Chou Chou in her arms. And then, when the Princess Pauline thrust her large red nose out from between the curtains of the sedan chair, Colette dropped Chou Chou and stood with her mouth agape!

This was the first time that she had really seen the Princess Pauline.

She was amazed to see that the Princess Pauline was not the beautiful, golden-haired, dainty-nosed little girl she had imagined all princesses to be.

Chou Chou, who had been asleep in Colette's arms, landed on the grass and stood blinking, still half-covered by the old shawl.

Again the Princess pointed her rather fat, bejewelled royal finger at Colette's favorite tree.

"There is the place," she shouted. "That is the perfect place."

Her sudden shout frightened little Chou Chou and she scampered away from under the shawl. Colette, who was still staring at the Princess Pauline, did not see Chou Chou go.

"One moment, your Royal Highness," said the Princess' personal doctor. "Please let me examine this place."

The Princess nodded her royal head.

The Princess' doctor looked around at the grass that surrounded the big oak tree. Then he looked carefully through a large glass at the trunk of the tree. He lifted his nose high and sniffed the air. And at last he drew out of his pocket a thermometer and a barometer. He held the thermometer and the barometer high in the air and he studied them a moment.

"Yes, you are correct, your Royal Highness," said the doctor. "This is the perfect place. There is no poison ivy or other dangerous growths anywhere. The air is clean and fresh. The temperature is just right, neither too hot nor too cold . . . too moist nor too dry. You are right, my Princess, this is the perfect place."

"Very well," said the Princess Pauline. "Then it is done . . . Mayor, see that the square is clear every morning. No one is to be permitted within one hundred yards of this tree while I have my morning repose . . . And you may clear the square right now . . . I would repose at once."

"Yes, your Royal Highness," whispered the Mayor as he bowed.

"And there must be silence as I repose," shouted the Princess. "Silence . . . silence . . . Absolute silence!"

Her voice had risen as she spoke. That last "silence" was loud enough to be heard throughout the little town of Grasse and across the valley.

"Yes, your Royal Highness," whispered the Mayor, very sadly.

The Mayor bowed deeply again. He worried and wondered . . . Where will the housewives do their marketing now? Where will the children play? . . . And where will the old men of the town discuss important topics?

But he said nothing. He promptly went around the square whispering the Princess' command to all the citizens of Grasse. The housewives and merchants grumbled in whispers as they picked up their packages and went home. The old men who sat on the wall around the square stood up, shook their heads, and frowned as they left the square. And little Colette gathered up her playthings and went home too.

Not one of the citizens of Grasse said anything out loud as they left the square.

But when the Mayor got home, there was a lot said. And it was said in a very loud hoarse whisper by the Mayor's wife.

"Royalty . . . *Poyalty!* . . . I don't care if she *is* a Royal Princess . . . Yes, your Royal Highness . . . No, your Royal Highness . . ." whispered the Mayor's wife angrily as she mimicked the voice of her husband, and bowed and curtsied. "No one has a right to take away our market place . . ."

"Shush, shush," whispered the Mayor . . . and he ran to shut the windows. "You're speaking treason."

"Treason . . . *Peason!*" whispered his angry wife. "If I cannot go to market . . . I cannot buy food. If I

25

cannot buy food . . . I cannot cook. If I cannot cook . . . we will starve . . . If we starve . . .''

At that moment little Colette pushed open the door into the kitchen.

"Has Chou Chou come home?" she asked. "She ran away in the square and I cannot find her."

"Oh, she's somewhere about," said her mother. "Maybe she's under the house . . . Look under the house."

Colette went out again and looked under the house. In a moment she was back again. The Mayor's wife was still whispering angrily to the Mayor. He held his hands over his ears.

"She's not there," said Colette.

"Who's not where?" said her mother.

"Chou Chou . . . you said she's under the house," said Colette.

"I said *maybe* she's under the house," said her mother. "Try the garden. You know where she likes to play . . . You will hear her somewhere in the garden, I'm sure."

"No . . . I don't think I will hear her in the garden," said Colette. "She is wearing the little pink woolen muzzle I knitted for her."

"Oh, that is true . . . Wait, I'll go with you. We will find the poor little thing even if she cannot cry out because of the dreadful muzzle she must wear for . . . Silence."

The Mayor's wife started for the door and then she turned and hissed at her husband.

"Silence . . . silence . . . Absolute silence!"

She shook her head and glared at the Mayor. And at last she followed Colette out the back door to the garden.

Colette and her mother looked high and low for Chou Chou, but found no sign of her.

"Oh, she must be off hunting grasshoppers or playing somewhere," said Colette's mother. "She will return before nightfall . . . Come to lunch now."

But little Chou Chou did not return that night . . . nor the next day or even the day after that.

Colette searched in vain for Chou Chou throughout the town. She asked everyone if he had seen her little kitten. But no one had seen her since the day the Princess Pauline first rode into the town square in her golden sedan chair. Little Colette had no time for play or anything else. She spent all her waking hours looking for her lost little Chou Chou.

The town of Grasse had settled back to its regular routine. The citizens suffered in silence the now unwelcome visit of Her Royal Highness Princess Pauline.

A temporary market place had been set up on the road a little distance away from the town square. There the unhappy housewives whispered together as they bought their daily food. And there the children of Grasse leaned silently against the wall that ran alongside the road. And there, too, the old men of the town sat glumly on the stone wall.

Yes, the people of Grasse were unhappy. And some of them were even angry. And the angriest one of all was the Mayor's wife. She would whisper angrily to other housewives in the market place. And then sometimes after she and some other housewives had bought their long breads at the baker's stall, she would lead the others past the town square. They all held their long breads upright like clubs . . . or swords!

The Mayor nervously watched them from a distance. He was afraid that the housewives, led by his own angry wife, would invade the square and attack the Princess as she reposed smugly in her golden sedan chair under Colette's favorite oak tree.

And now the blacksmith, who had stopped pounding his anvil; the carpenter, who had stopped sawing wood and hammering nails; the shoemaker, candlemaker, and all the others who had stopped doing their work because of the laws of silence . . . just twiddled their thumbs as they sat on the low stone wall near the road market place with the old men.

The old men whispered unhappily about the topics of the day. But the blacksmith, the carpenter, and all the others did not whisper . . . They just sat silently, unhappily, twiddling their thumbs. They were men of action, not words.

Perhaps the Mayor of Grasse was the unhappiest man in the whole town. He missed the sound of cowbells, the sound of children playing in the square, the cheerful sound of housewives gossiping in the market place, and men cheerfully working at their tasks. He even missed the clatter of wooden shoes on the cobblestones and the barking of dogs and mewing of cats.

He avoided the eyes of all the townspeople as he

walked the streets. And at home he dared not look into
the sad eyes of little Colette (who missed her kitten
Chou Chou dreadfully) . . . and he tried to drown out
the hoarse, angry whispering of his wife by wearing
his wig well down around his ears.

He racked his brain for some scheme that would end
the visit of the Princess Pauline . . . or at least hurry it
along. At last, on the third morning of the Princess'
visit, something happened that solved his problem.

About midmorning on that day the Princess again
sent an urgent message to the Mayor of Grasse. She
demanded that he come at once to the place she had
chosen for her morning's repose under the shade of
Colette's favorite oak tree in the corner of the square.

The Mayor hurried from his house to obey the Princess' command. Many of the housewives and the old
men and children followed him and stood at a discreet
distance when he bowed to the Princess.

The Princess Pauline was very angry!

"So you've come at last," shouted the Princess.

30

"I came as soon as I received your message, your Royal Highness," whispered the Mayor as he bowed deeply.

"Very well . . . very well," said the Princess impatiently. "Did I not command that there be silence . . . absolute silence during my morning's repose? . . ."

"Yes, your Royal Highness," whispered the Mayor.

"Very well, then . . . be silent and listen," commanded the Princess.

The Mayor was silent. And everyone else was silent. No one breathed.

Somewhere nearby the Mayor could hear a faint "Meow."

"There," shouted the Princess. "Did you hear it?

. . . Cats yowling! . . . Cats yowling all over the place
. . . Listen again."

Again the Mayor listened and everyone else listened
too. Again they heard "Meow . . . Meow" very faintly.

"That's it . . . Now, sir Mayor, what will you do
about that horrible noise that is disturbing my morning
repose?" demanded the Princess Pauline.

"Your Royal Highness," whispered the Mayor, "all
our cats have been muzzled. Perhaps some strange cat
has come to Grasse . . ."

Little Colette, who had been standing with her mother
out on the road while her father spoke to the Princess,
suddenly ran on tiptoe across the square. She curtsied
to the Princess (as she had been taught to do in school),
then she tugged at the Mayor's coat. She wanted to tell
him something. The Mayor bent down and Colette
whispered into his ear.

"It is Chou Chou, Papa. It must be Chou Chou up
in the tree . . . I'm sure it is. She must have pushed her
muzzle off and she's crying . . . Oh, look, I can see her
now, sitting on one of the highest branches."

"Have no fear, my child. Chou Chou will be rescued,"
whispered the Mayor into Colette's ear.

Then the Mayor straightened up and peered up into
the oak tree.

"What is it? What has happened? . . . Stop staring
into the sky and do something about the yowling cats,"
shouted the Princess.

"Your Royal Highness," whispered the Mayor after he had bowed again, "I have just been informed that a cat over which I have no control is up in the tree above your royal head . . . in a few minutes she will . . ."

"Oh . . . Oh . . . A cat uncontrolled! . . . A wildcat . . . a wildcat over my head ready to spring . . . Save me," screamed Princess Pauline. "Save me . . ."

"Save Her Royal Highness," roared the Princess' doctor.

"Save the Royal Princess," shouted the Princess' servants.

The huge chairmen rushed to Princess Pauline's sedan chair. They lifted the chair and ran as fast as they could from the square and up the road. Princess Pauline rattled about in her sedan chair like a loose pea in a pod.

And racing after the Princess and the chair was her doctor, her servants, and at last the Mayor of Grasse, still whispering as loud as he dared.

"Your Royal Highness . . . Stop . . . stop . . . Your Royal Highness, there's been a mistake . . . Stop . . . stop . . ."

But the huge chairmen carrying Princess Pauline's sedan chair did not stop. They were as afraid of wildcats as the Princess was. And they ran up the road as fast as they could go until they had left the town of Grasse behind them. They stopped at last, but only because they had run up a long steep hill and could run no more. They set the Princess' sedan chair down none too gently on the top of the hill and they both collapsed right in the road.

The Mayor, who was completely out of breath, finally
labored to the top of the hill.

"Your Royal Highness," he gasped, "there has been
a mistake . . ."

The Princess Pauline thrust her head out from behind the curtains of her sedan chair. She had been so
shaken and tumbled about during that mad dash up the
hill that her crown hung over one eye and the many
necklaces she wore were tangled in a scrambled knot
around her throat.

37

"What was that? . . . What did you? . . . Hold! . . . Be silent . . ." shouted the Princess.

She was now looking beyond the Mayor. She turned her head slowly and she looked up and around.

"Behold . . . What have we here?" she cried. "*These* are oak trees! . . . True oak trees! . . . Larger trees than any of the puny trees in your town of Grasse. Here are great spreading oaks, a grove of them. Yes, this shall be the place for my morning repose . . . the perfect place."

The Princess' doctor quickly examined with his glass, his nose, and his thermometer and barometer the new place that she had chosen for her repose. He agreed it was the perfect place . . . a much finer, safer, even healthier place than the one she had chosen in the town square.

"Then it is done . . . Sir Mayor, I will have no further need of the town of Grasse," said the Princess Pauline haughtily. "I shall live in some nearby chalet and I shall repose here every morning in silence . . . absolute silence!"

"Yes, your Royal Highness," whispered the Mayor with a sigh of relief. Then he took a deep breath and went on, "Your Royal Highness, as Mayor of Grasse it is with deep regret . . ." (It was obvious the Mayor was going to make a speech of farewell . . . a long speech.)

"Spare me your long-winded farewells," shouted the Princess. "I would repose at once . . . Sir Mayor, I bid you adieu . . . I want silence . . . you hear! Absolute silence!"

"Yes, your Royal Highness," whispered the Mayor. And he bowed deeper than ever to keep the Princess from seeing the happy relief in his eyes.

Then the Mayor hurried down the hill. When he was safely out of sight of the Princess he ventured a little skip or two. And a little further on his way, he danced a step . . . then he skipped . . . And he danced and skipped, skipped and danced all the way back to town.

He was so happy that the citizens of Grasse were free once more to talk out loud, to dance and sing, and make all the cheerful noises (within reason) anyone wanted to make.

He was happy, too, that bells could ring again, that

doors and cartwheels could squeak again . . . that children could bounce their balls, that the blacksmith could
pound his anvil and the carpenter could saw his wood
. . . that the housewives could market and gossip in
the town square and that even dogs, cats, and donkeys
could bark, meow, and bray freely . . . And that everyone could make the cheerful noises they must make to
live happily in the town of Grasse.

When the Mayor reached the town square he found
that the good people of Grasse had lost no time in getting
little Chou Chou out of the big oak. She was welcomed
down in the town square as a great heroine. The people
cheered, clapped their hands, and bowed and curtsied.

41

Great bowls of milk and cream and all sorts of good things (like more milk and cream) were brought to the poor hungry little kitten. In a few minutes she had lapped up so much milk and cream she was as round as a furry ball and she fell fast asleep in Colette's arms.

Right then and there the Mayor of Grasse declared a holiday. All through the day the fiddlers played and the people and the children sang and danced. And just at sunset all the felt slippers the people had worn to keep their shoes from clattering on the pavement, all the bundles of straw they had wrapped around the hooves of their horses and donkeys . . . all the padding and safeguards that had been used so that there would be "Silence . . . silence . . . Absolute silence . . ." were piled up in the center of the town square.

And on the top of the pile was placed (by the Mayor of Grasse himself) the long paper he had posted in the square listing the laws of silence. And on top of that he placed the tiny pink woolen muzzle that Chou Chou had worn.

Then he put a torch to the huge pile.

What a wonderful bonfire *that* was!

And all the people and children of Grasse joined hands and danced and sang around the great bonfire until it had burned down to embers.

Then the Mayor made a speech in which he called Chou Chou the Joan of Arc of Kittendom.

(He did not explain that sentence but the old men of the town understood what he meant and they nodded.)

At long last everyone went home, clattering on the cobblestone streets in their wooden shoes or hobnailed boots. They went home to sleep and snore (if they would) with no concern for the laws of silence anymore.

The grateful citizens of Grasse never forgot the good service that little Chou Chou, Colette's kitten, had performed for their town.

A little bronze plaque was made and nailed to the oak tree wherein brave little Chou Chou had spent three days and two nights alone . . . hungry . . . and frightened.

On the bronze plaque under a portrait of Chou Chou, made by the town blacksmith, were these immortal words:

In Honor

of

Chou Chou

Whose Great Courage

And Boundless Fortitude

Rendered an Unforgettable Service

to

The People of Grasse

Unfortunately, the great oak with its bronze plaque was struck by lightning many years after that and there is no longer any sign of the tree and the plaque that honored Chou Chou.

But she has not been forgotten by the grateful citizens of Grasse.

Since then any kitten born in Grasse who shows any exceptional courage . . . when chasing flies or stalking grasshoppers . . . is promptly named Chou Chou in honor of the first great Chou Chou.

46

And the Princess Pauline has not been forgotten either. The great grove of oak trees . . . where Princess Pauline reposed every morning after she left the town square . . . is still there.

That great grove of oak trees is now called Princess Pauline's garden . . . but the people of Grasse rarely go there.

They usually say, "Today is too hot a day to climb a long hill" . . . And most days are hot in Grasse.

Another reason the people of Grasse rarely go there is that there is silence in and around Princess Pauline's Garden . . . an unpleasant silence . . . an Absolute Silence!